HAPPY BEES!

by Arthur Yorinks
Illustrated by Carey Armstrong-Ellis

Harry N. Abrams, Inc., Publishers

Happy bees

even the fleas love 'em

how could you not
as big as a dot
buzzing around a lot.

Happy bees
even the weeds love 'em

fly through the air
and rest on a bear
what a life!
these happy bees.

Happy bees
how
could
you
not
love 'em
days without care
with nothing to wear

what a life!
these happy bees.

Happy bees
stinging knees

sailing the seas

munching Swiss cheese

sleeping in trees
sounding like Zs . . .

and forget
their tissues
whenever they sneeze.

mmmmAHCHOOom

Happy bees
both hes and shes
live in Belize
or wherever they please

Happy bees
what a life!
these happy bees.

everyone loves 'em

bumbling

tumbling

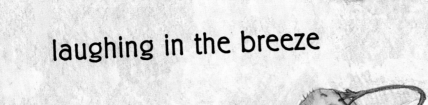

laughing in the breeze

what a life
we all should have
like happy bees.

For Anka
—A. Y.

To Amo, my "bestest" friend
—C. A. E.

Medium: Gouache and colored pencil

Design by Edward Miller
Production Manager: Jonathan Lopes

Library of Congress Cataloging-in-Publication Data

Yorinks, Arthur.
Happy bees / by Arthur Yorinks ; illustrated by Carey Armstrong-Ellis.
p. cm.
Summary: Rhythmic text describes the carefree life of bees as they sting knees, munch on Swiss cheese, and laugh in the breeze.
ISBN 0-8109-5866-X
[1. Bees—Fiction. 2. Stories in rhyme.] I. Armstrong-Ellis, Carey, ill. II. Title.

PZ8.3.Y765Hap 2005
[E]—dc22
2004015454

Printed and bound in China
1 3 5 7 9 10 8 6 4 2

Harry N. Abrams, Inc.
100 Fifth Avenue
New York, NY 10011
www.abramsbooks.com

Abrams is a subsidiary of

LA MARTINIÈRE
GROUPE